I HEARD THE BELLS...

NOW AND THEN

Published and sold by
www.Amazon.com

2020

DEDICATED to all those who support my life goals, they know who they are.

SYNOPSIS

This is a story of survival and growth. After enduring over a decade of physical and mental abuse Pippa is brought to the depths of despair. Nevertheless feeling abandoned by the universe and God (if he existed), manages to finally escape the violence, but Pippa still finds herself alone with overwhelming responsibilities of a family she is ill equipped to deal with on her own still being but a child herself. Until that is, two strangers knock on her door and her life sets off in a new direction, one of hope, direction and lifelong education. They teach her about her origins and purpose in life. Soon she is adopted into a worldwide extended gospel family eager to help her reach her true potential. They help her learn to forgive, overcome bitterness and social ineptness, she finds a true friend who helps her develop still further in her personal success and independence, something she never could have allowed herself to dream she was capable of before.

Although this is a work of fiction it has been based on real events and experiences. And dedicated to the untold stories of the abuse cycle some people get trapped in. Not all of them have a Cinderella endings as the news of violent deaths are still common in the media. Abuse does come in cycles I have observed because, one may escape an abuser but then having low self -esteem, and vulnerability attracts other abusers who target them knowing they will be swept off their feet by a kind word!!

So what about all those little success stories you never hear about? Just putting one's life back together after the trauma of spousal abuse and sometimes very much against all odds, is a major achievement that takes courage, patience and a lot of hard work and yes sometimes therapy. They are the quiet warriors of this world and deserve our admiration. To anyone this book resonates with I admire you, applaud you and wish you all the best.

You are not alone nor should you feel your success is diminished by the great success stories you hear about, you are no less successful, or worthy of recognition.

<u>CONTENTS</u>   <u>PAGE</u>

CONTENTS   PAGE

CHAPTER 1

"I am not sure I can do this Lissy, what have I got myself into?"

Lissy (short for Elizabeth) giggled and leant over the small cining table and her long blond hair fell forward and stroked the table as she looked Pippa right in the eyes, her face turning serious, 'Of course you can, I have faith in you'.

Pippa drew back into her chair and her uncertainty felt almost overwhelming

"I have never done anything like this before or mixed with these types of people, what do I know about running a stately home? I will be sacked within days!" she exclaimed raising her arms in despair and letting them drop heavily onto the table in front of her!

"It's not rocket science, you can organise a home and office, you will be shown the ropes and you can follow a recipe that's basically all it is."

Pippa was less than convinced and Lissy continued

"They were impressed with your CV and you aced the interview so they think you're ideal for the job, they liked you, not only that I will be at the end of the phone if you need help."

"I don't know what I was thinking to let you talk me into this."

Lissy pressed home her point in earnest knowing her friend simply lacked confidence in herself, years of being put down and oppressed by a controlling husband, had done that to her until she had finally made the break in 1985, the years since had healed a lot but some scars like lack of confidence did not heal so easily.

"You knew it made sense and one of the few chances to make an actual good wage, at our ages starting at the beginning after rearing a family does not allow too many options for careers without years of study, by which time there's not much time to develop a decent pension or savings plan. You spent 6 months catching up with the work scene by studying office admin but what would you get paid in an office starting as a junior? Less the £5 an hour, not even enough to live on let alone save or pay into a pension. This is a life changing opportunity for you and what is the worst that can happen?"

"I can think of loads of bad scenarios." Pippa announced, but before she could list any Lissy assured her she would be fine and promised to be there to fetch her home if things got too much. This seemed to reassure Pippa somewhat and she began to settle down emotionally and accept this really was a good opportunity for someone in her position. She had too many wasted years being married to someone who did not value or cherish her, to make up for and this job may be just what she needed at this time. A new beginning. Now that her children had all left home she was also feeling the emptiness and loneliness quite acutely.

Lissy got up and gathered their cups from the table and took them to the sink, and began rinsing them up.

"We will have another hot drink and then go and look at some clothes in town you will need some decent clothes at least."

Pippa smiled if all went well with the new job she would be able to finally afford nice things for herself which was something she had never experienced before, her friend had offered to treat her to new clothes just for the start of her new life, Pippa had objected at first but Lissy was very persuasive and pointed out that Pippa would do the same for her. Satisfied she had made her point and had reassured her friend, Lissy then filled the kettle and flicked the switch and sat down again facing Pippa who by now was feeling a bit more settled and had begun to look forward to her new adventure, and that was what she had just then decided, she was going to treat her soon to be new circumstances as an adventure. 'Yes.' she thought resolutely

"This will be my adventure." Pippa had not realised she had said this out loud until Lissy replied....

"That's the ticket."

With this little thought in her mind she began to feel quite excited and her fears were quelled at least for the moment as she looked forward to the new chapter of her life.

The friends spent the next half hour or so discussing clothes and making plans which shops to visit first and what might be suitable attire.

Lissy knew about these things because she had been a nanny for titled and rich people for quite a few years or so not having had any children herself, and this seemed the best job she could ever think of. She had built for herself quite a good reputation amongst the young parents in those circles and it was her reputation she had used to convince the agency to consider Pippa for the new posting. She was known for her integrity and Pippa having the same values and integrity it was not hard to convince them.

As the women prepared to go out and gathered handbags and coats from the hall, Lissy suddenly had a thought as she turned the latch to open the door, "By the way, what will you do about church on Sundays?

Pippa grinned, "They told me I had one day off a week so I told them it had to be Sunday which they seemed quite happy with that, and my explanation it was for religious reasons that I did not work on Sundays, they actually seemed impressed with that."

Lissy smiled her pride and approval of her friend then turned to lead Pippa out of the door and waited for Pippa to lock it behind them. Lissy knew that had the couple objected to that stipulation Pippa would have had no hesitation in refusing the job outright! In some ways Pippa was stronger than she realised and standing up for her gospel principles was one of them, maybe because it was the one thing in her life she felt sure of. Which was something Lissy herself never had the gall to do and Lissy admired Pippa for it.

CHAPTER 2

Lissy was born in Denver, Colorado, when her parents died in an accident when she was just 21 she felt she needed a change after several months of grieving. So when she finished her training and had become a qualified nanny, she had had a couple of short placements in her local area, when a more permanent position opened up in London just at the time she felt was right to move on from her grief, She signed up to an international agency, which opened up new horizons and was an exciting opportunity for her and paid really good money. So that is how she ended up in England.

It was through singles weekend events organised through the church they both belonged to that Pippa and Lissy had met and become great friends. They lived quite far apart but that did not matter nor did it matter that after attending these events now for several years they were both still single and not for want of trying! Lissy was far more outgoing and sociable than Pippa, and slowly over the past few years Lissy had managed to tease Pippa out of her shell somewhat. This had come to fruition when Pippa's children had all left home leaving her with a void that needed filling and Lissy jumped at the opportunity to expand her friends Pippa's horizons and help her get a life after being trodden down by other people in her life up to then.

Lissy had always had self- confidence and had no trouble with her ambitious plans for her future. She had not got this far in life by being a wilting violet! She was pretty much the top of her game by this time and had been head hunted by wealthy families on occasion for her skills as a nanny to the upper class families she worked for always gave her top recommendations. She enjoyed status and certain perks she had come to expect in her work, like holidays with the families in exotic locations, use of swimming pools on her clients property and when her work took her to homes with stables she even got to ride horses, which was something she knew Pippa would have loved.

Lissy was almost opposite to Pippa as she was very conscious of fashion and makeup and often she would instigate - girls nights where they would pamper each other and it would give Lissy an excuse to introduce Pippa to makeup and nice clothes, as they were both similar height and build, however Lissy had long curly blond hair again opposite to Pippa who's hair was as straight as a die but in silky smooth condition adding to her younger looks. Lissy was quite stunning when she was made up, she had delicate features, green eyes and her clothes were clearly quality and tailored, accentuating her figure beautifully. She had great taste and Pippa often commented on and admired her for that.

Lissy was keenly aware of the struggles Pippa had experienced and was determined to help her friend realise her potential and have the life she thought her friend deserved. This dynamic created a close bond that the women appreciated and needed at that time. Lissy still mourned her losses as a child of her parents and missed them terribly and Pippa filled part of the gap they had left in her heart, and it was getting a little late in life to be thinking of starting her own family as that was one of the sacrifices she had made for her career, she had never had time to create her own family.

Pippa on the other hand had married very early and was barely 17 when she had had her first child. The marriage lasted only ten years and 3 kids later she found herself a single parent with very little to look forward to. She had left school with very few basic qualifications as she had the romantic notion her husband would take care of her!

That dream brutally shattered by violence and mental cruelty, and messy divorce, she had begun to educate herself whilst at the same time rearing her children in preparation for the time she knew would come when she had to be independent. She had been very lucky to have the support of her church friends who encouraged her to grow and especially Lissy whom she loved as a sister. She had had many part time menial jobs that fit in with kids schedules but now she was not only looking at full time work but a live in job and that scared her, and excited her at the same time, she was not shy of hard work, just not confident of her abilities. However she had a back- up plan in case things went wrong, she would sublet her tiny flat to her youngest daughter rather than sell up, so Pippa had somewhere to return to if things went wrong and her daughter who was at university at that time had a safe cheap place to live. If things did work out Pippa thought she would revisit her options then.

CHAPTER 3

As her start date got closer Pippa got more nervous and restless

Before starting her new adventure Lissy insisted Pippa should stay with her for a couple of days so that they could celebrate together. Pippa loved her friend for her consideration but she would have much preferred to be at home and to get her head together, or maybe Lissy knew she would worry herself if she left her alone! So Pippa packed the night before and was sitting at the table having breakfast thinking of how the events that were about to change her life had come about whilst she waited for her friend to pick her up.

Pippa was middle aged and still quite young looking to say she had three grown children, she was medium built but had never really gotten into the makeup and clothes scene so rarely used makeup which she did not really need anyway as her skin had a healthy glow under a mop of auburn hair which she kept neatly in a plain shoulder length bob, simple and easy to keep which pretty much summed her up! She was not one to fuss about her appearance so long as she was neat and clean that was as far as her fashion interests went. Pippa had been through a lot in her life and she was now hoping to start a new chapter and be able to close the book on her old life. Of course that did not include her children whom she loved dearly but this time was her time, a time to define who she really wanted to be. She was barely a teenager when she got married and had children so had never really thought about who or what she wanted to be as an individual. She had little in the way of academic qualifications other than what she had recently acquired and so felt very blessed to be having this opportunity to prove herself. The only encouragement to achieve anything for herself had come from the association with the members of the church

she joined fifteen or more years ago. The
Church of Jesus Christ of Latter-day Saints, as
it is called was a major influence on her life, it
gave her purpose and helped her regain her
self- esteem when life (before she found her
faith) had practically destroyed it. It was
where she had met one of her best friends
Lissy.

Now here she was preparing to
embark on an adventure most people could
only dream of.

Pippa needed to get a job after rearing
her children alone and she had tried to
prepare for that time by familiarising herself
with a computer and office work and had
even done an NVQ 3 in business admin.,
which she felt she could confidently do. She
had successfully completed work placements
but what she had not anticipated was the low
wages especially going in as a junior which in
spite of her age that would be what she was.
She had discussed this dilemma with Lissy as

there was no way even doing forty to fifty hours a week at £4.50 an hour she could live on such a small income it barely covered her rent let alone anything else. Pippa was fearful for her future. She was frugal and making the budget stretch had become a necessary skill she excelled in but even she could not stretch such a low budget that far!

It was about that time that Lissy suggested signing up to an agency as a housekeeper, and promised Pippa to look into the possibility of signing up to her own agency as she was quite respected in those circles and had a good rapport with the manager. The thought had quite excited the pair of friends as they brainstormed all the possibilities and the freedom a good wage would afford Pippa. Lissy even threw in a long term plan to encourage her friend to have a long term goal.

"If we both save" Lissy began "we could go into business ourselves and open a guest house together."   With a sharp intake of breath Pippa replied

"You would really like to do that with me?"

"Why not? We work together really well"

"That would be fantastic I would love that, and doing a housekeeping job would pretty much train me on the job so to speak, and you have great people skills already."

"Exactly what I was thinking, we would have the option to buy here or abroad where prices are so much cheaper, I speak French so language would not be a barrier and I am sure you would pick it up quick enough"

"What about my kids though?"

"We could discuss that nearer the time they may even want to move with us but one step at a time it would just take us longer if we buy in Britain but hopefully we can do this before we both hit fifty!."

They both laughed.

CHAPTER 4

Pippa started out of her revelries by the sound of the doorbell and she stood up from the table and went tc answer the door thinking to herself "She's early I am not ready." but as she opened the door she realised her mistake it was just the postman with a small parcel for a neighbour so after explaining to him that she would be going out she closed the door, and she returned to the dining room.

"Phew." she thought as she cleared away her breakfast things still thinking of how she had got to this point in her life. Her friends at church thought she was brave and when she asked a couple of them to give her references to give her employers they were more than happy to assist as in her own little way Pippa had made an impression on them as being honest and reliable and they had no qualms about supporting her application, and writing references, and wished her all the best. Pippa had explained to her bishop when he spoke to her. "I am keeping on my flat and subletting it, so my home will still be rooted here and I shall be back for holidays and to visit my family."

"How does your family feel about you going away?" he had asked from the other side of his large wooden desk in his office.

"I don't think they believe it really, they cannot envisage their unremarkable Mum is really capable of holding the job down and able to mingle with people they regard as toffs" she laughed and he joined in the humour

"And you are going to prove them wrong, I have faith in you, you just have to believe in yourself. I remember when I first met you wouldn't say boo to a goose! You were so far into your shell you almost disappeared as a person and I am glad to have been privileged to witness your growth."

"I could not have grown without my faith in the Lord and the help people have given me over the years, let's face it Bishop I was just a kid and barely able to organise my own home when the missionaries knocked on my door, I was a single parent and totally overwhelmed. I will always be grateful to those two young men who gave up two years of their lives to do the Lords work, had they not found me who knows what would have happened to us as I was at the end of my tether and they came in answer to my prayers. When I came to church I so appreciated the sisters who took me under their wing and taught me how to cook and run my home and look after 3 small traumatised children. I loved the companionship they gave me and the activities we shared. I am sure I frustrated a few of them with my lack of knowledge and neediness but they persevered with me" Pippa giggled at the memory.

"Look how far you have come Pippa"

"Yeah, I really did not have a clue about kids, but look at them now, all at University who would have thought it I am so proud of them, and given our circumstances and poverty that too is a miracle and only made possible with help from ward members filling the gaps their absent father left in his wake"

"Well that's what the Lord would want us to do and hopefully you will have opportunities to help others as I know that is your nature. I know you will do well, Pippa and we are all still here when you visit so keep in touch, and don't underestimate yourself you have overcome a lot"

As the conversation was coming to a natural close he stood up and offered her his hand and she returned the gesture by giving his a hearty shake and they both smiled, he was tall and towered over her as he moved around the desk to usher her to the door "Good luck and don't forget to call on the priesthood if you need them." Were his parting words.

That was not her last interview but it was the one she remembered most.

Her new position caused a lot of chatter amongst the members as it was not the run of the mill job and Pippa was the most unlikely candidate and that tickled many of them as it did herself it was like being the main character in a Catherine Cookson novel!

Her thoughts returned to the here and now and Pippa looked at her watch, it was almost time Lissy had planned to arrive so she had a last check around the flat that everything was in order including the list of instructions for her daughter she left in the middle of the table (which included relevant phone numbers Pippa thought she might need), with care instructions for plants etc. She checked her appearance in the full length mirror in the hall, adjusted some stray hairs with her hand and pulled on her navy skirt suit top to straighten some creases then went to the door and set the latch so that Lissy could walk straight in, then she entered the living room and got on her knees to pray for courage. She was there for about 5 minutes when got the distinct impression in her mind *"You can do this."* Which she recognised as coming from the Holy Spirit and in response she replied "I get it, I have to suck it up, and take a deep breath." She thought in response. She closed her prayer and got up, it wasn't long before she heard a familiar voice, calling from the hall "Where are you? You ready for this?"

"I'm here in the living room, and yes I am ready." She called back. "But are they ready for me!" she thought jokingly.

CHAPTER 5

In order to understand the miracle of Pippa's new life and achievement, it is necessary to at least give a brief inkling of the horrors she endured to get to that point in her life that became an adventure in personal growth. The pain and despair covered at least a decade, and change was not instant, that too took more years of hard work and determination. Her life could be summed up now however, with her favourite carol in her hymn book. *'I Heard The Bells On Christmas Day'.*   A cry of despair culminating in a song of hope.

She grew up in a single parent home in a poor Scottish city centre slum tenements. Most people there were quite poor they had food and clothes but not much else. People there rarely took holidays but those who did would hire a caravan for a self-catering affair. Her mother worked all hours to keep the roof over their heads and pay a sitter for Pippa and Elise her sister. Their father having left while they were still young. Life was not easy but the girls made what they could of the situation and since most of the people around them were just as poor, the girls themselves did not feel at all different. They could amuse themselves with very little a comic Friday nights on their mums payday was the highlight of their week along with a small ice cream block between them which they plopped into a glass of lemonade to make ice cream sodas, and they delighted in watching the froth appear and having to drink the lemonade through the fluffy cloud that got up their noses as they did so.

To earn pocket money the girls would collect glass pop and beer bottles and would return them to the off licence who paid for their return. During the summer they would wait outside the nearby church for the end of a wedding service they knew to be in progress, and blend in with the guests when they emerged, because it was customary for

the groom to throw coppers into the well-
wishing crowd of guests as they proceeded to
the waiting car or carriage. The girls could
pick up to two shillings off the pavement
where they the tinkling coins fell, but usually
they managed an average of about sixpence
in ha'pennies (half pennies).

They were not the only children to do
this so competition could be quite fierce as
they all scrabbled between the adults' legs as
they jostled in order to hail and audibly
congratulate the newlyweds!

It was not until they moved to
Yorkshire mining town that the gap between
their circumstances and the normal working
class began to isolate them and they began to
feel the weight of their circumstance and
experience class distinction and prejudice.
Often being poor and their 'foreign' accents
made them objects of ridicule. Pippa was
quick to learn to speak with a Yorkshire twang
but it was too late and the other kids labelled

her Haggis anyway and it stuck at least through primary school!

It was much harder to earn pocket money as off licenses in Yorkshire did not pay for bottles. There were no wedding coin rituals either so that was disappointing. Elise seemed to adjust better than Pippa and could hold her own with the help of her new found friends. But Pippa internalised the insults and changes.

By the time Pippa went to secondary school she was overwhelmed with the animosity around her and could not make friends easily which made her an even bigger target for bullying. Her world seemed to shrink to the four walls of her tiny bedroom. Never having dealt with this phenomena before she had no way of protecting herself. She was not a fighter and was completely at the mercy of bullies. Day by day she became more and more miserable and lonely, she engaged very little with her family and appeared to them to become a typically anti - social teenager!

She had always been a bit of a tomboy, always up for adventure and no fear of consequences. This often landed her in trouble as it did one day when she brought a 'poor pussycat' home (Scottish Wildcat as was later identified from a book) for her mum to feed! She had no fear of animals and even brought wild animals home that she had found as though they were long time pets of hers and they seemed to have no fear of her, but her mother was not so lucky and would often be scratched and bitten by them before she was able to eject them from their home!

She had never really had any fear of people either but this was different, it was confrontational and incessant name calling, mockery, being set up to fight and ever more serious threats to her life. Every day she felt as though she was running the gauntlet, hiding from her assailants and living in constant fear and rejection and ridicule. She could never understand what it was she had done to any of them that would make them hate her so much. Nothing was sacred to them, they made fun of everything about her, her intelligence, her thin lanky body, her hair, everything. Anyone who has ever been bullied at school will know how soul destroying it becomes day in and day out like psychological torture, it was relentless. Often the group of girl bullies who were particularly cruel, would gather in great groups of their friends and wait for her outside the school gates at the end of the school day. Like people gathering to see a dog fight the crowd would swell and chatter in excitement and anticipation of the event. Teachers were quite aware of these events and would escort her through them until she was far enough away from the crowd to run the rest of the two miles home. This would not be tolerated in schools today but back in the late 70's this particular school seemed to accept these practices and not take them seriously. Needless to say she became fear-full of everyone and everything and her life became almost paralysed in an eternal round of self-doubt, fear, and inability to function.

Over the years Pippa did try different things to protect herself, she became a librarian and would feel safe amongst the rows of books she loved in the school, and stayed in at break times to avoid being exposed in the playground which worked for a while. Now and again she had a little peace but the threat was always there hanging over her head like a guillotine and inevitably she would be found and the onslaught would begin again.

She stopped having showers after games and PE, and eventually refused to do games at all, because the other girls would throw her clothes into the showers and mock her undeveloped body and during the games would knock her over or hit her with hockey sticks when the teacher was not looking which seemed all too often in Pippa's mind!. She had to defy the teachers to do it but by then Pippa was desperate and would rather face the teacher's wrath than the bullies' cruelty. Her mother supported her but ultimately felt helpless because Pippa insisted that if she interfered it would just make things worse and as time went on she began to become more reclusive and stopped telling her mother because she felt it was all so hopeless there was nothing anyone could do. Her mother naturally thought her efforts to address the problem had some success since she was getting fewer complaints from Pippa herself.

Pippa's schoolwork took a noticeable nosedive as her concentration lapsed, all she could think about all day was how to be invisible or working out a stratagem to get home safely. Finally Pippa could take the isolation, the feeling of being different, and hated, her thoughts became desperate and dark, she felt she could not live another day in her misery, her life seemed pointless and so deeply miserable, there seemed no relief in sight. So one evening when her mother was at a neighbours and she was not expecting her to return any time soon, she took the opportunity to raid the bathroom cabinet and tearfully helped herself to every pill and potion she thought could help her end this eternal misery. She even considered her family would be better off without her. Finally she felt she was taking control, that she was going somewhere where she could never be hurt again. *"Nothingness, no painful thoughts, no facing hatred and mockery, no feelings of loneliness, uselessness, being a freak that everyone hated, no misery, I will just sleep in peace and not have to face anyone ever again."* For the first time in years she felt she was finally in control of her circumstances.

The Christmas Carol described the despair she had felt and the lack of peace around her. It was as though the author of this song knew her, knew her pain and despair, and seen the light and hope that she also finally found.

Eventually she would write her own version of the Carol which begins thus.

<u>**SONG OF HOPE Part 1**</u>

The song of hope

Had missed my ears

As deafness claimed

My former years

Darkness meant

I could not see

The straight path

In front of me

Despair and anguish

Wrought my soul

Void of love

No heart was whole............

CHAPTER 6

Bleakstone Manor was an impressive mansion nestled in a valley in the Yorkshire Pennines. A far cry from Pippa's little ground floor flat in a little village in a north Yorkshire. It had been in the Buchanan family for centuries and Lord Rupert and Lady Beatrice Buchanan (Lord Bee and Lady Bee as spoken of by staff) were the last of their line as they had but two girls who would not be able to keep the family name when they married so in essence they were the last of their line which was one of Lady Bees bug bares.

The two girls lived and worked in London where all the action and limelight was and came home for some holidays bringing some of their wealthy titled friends to show off their home. From what Pippa could glean from her conversations with Lady Bee that they were struggling to keep things going and had had to sell some of the land to the council in order to get planning permission for expansion and money to expand. The Wedding events were fairly new and had unexpectedly taken off hence Ellen gave up housekeeping to concentrate on that side of her work and was now putting Pippa through her paces, or at least that was what was supposed to happen but her availability was limited so often that if Pippa rang for advice she was met with a certain hostility for interrupting her at work!

Nevertheless Pippa was able to work out her main duties herself and get into a fairly good routine by making notes and typing up daily rotas she could refer to and 'how to instructions' as many things were done in exact ways and at exact times such as breakfast trays for newly- weds, they had to be arranged just so with glass bowls of strawberries, cream jug champagne glasses and cooled little bottles of champagne, and a single rose in a little vase right at the centre.

Lady Bee often gave her notes and instructions which at first were very helpful in helping Pippa know what to do and when, however once she became experienced and knew what she was doing they became an irritation because often they were notes telling her to do things she had already done but to satisfy the lady t she would redo them such as polishing the brass door handles which she knew she had done the day before but Lady Bee insisted had not been done and this made Pippa doubt herself. So Pippa came up with yet another tick sheet recording the days she polished the brass so that there was no doubt in her mind that the job had been done and when.

Lord Bee spent most of his days in the estate offices which had been added to the north wing, and Ebony his black retriever was always by his side so Pippa rarely saw either of them once she had delivered his morning coffee to his office first thing in the morning, except for mealtimes. He was always the first of the office staff to arrive it was Pippa's Job to unlock the outer coors for them, collect the milk, post and paper. She would deposit the milk in the kitchen fridge, sort the post into personal and office piles, and deposit the post into the appropriate trays on the hall table just outside the offices and the personal post in the breakfast room along with the paper. Then she would make the coffee and deliver it to Lord Bee who was always so engrossed in his work he did not even acknowledge its arrival, however Ebony who was settled in her little bed near the door would look up and wag her tail, and Pippa would respond with a loving smile and bent over and gave her a tickle behind the ears before leaving the room. Pippa liked dogs but never had the stomach to clean up after them so that was what put her off owning one herself.

As for the cooking and menus she had plenty of cook books to refer to and she could at least follow a recipe which was definitely a saving grace. She often felt out of her depth but prayer and methodical thinking got her through a lot of it. She knew if she was to grow into this part she needed patience with herself and others and to keep calm and think things through before responding to new experiences. She also had the gospel to guide her in a lot of things and gave her confidence to keep her own standards, within the work for instance she would not work on Sundays and nothing would stop her keeping that standard and it also made sure she could not be put upon on her only day off. Pippa was always willing to go the extra mile to please especially at work so she knew the boundary was as much for herself as for her boss!

Pippa kept in touch with family and friends mainly by phone in the evenings after work.

Lady Bee she was to discover would test and stretch her to her limits on many of her standards and although they were an inconvenience to Lacy Bee she grew to respect Pippa's resolve making their relationship a little more on equal terms.

Pippa had expected life to be different to say the least but she really had not known what she was stepping into with this particular family. She had already decided to be somewhat aloof and keep her relationships strictly professional as much as she could before she even got there because she realised it would be hard to work out boundaries in that sort of situation, living in someone else's home. She had seen enough movies and read enough books to know that a life in service walked a fine line between professionalism and familiarity with the family, and she was determined not to cross that line.

This was going to prove much harder than she thought because Lady Bee was a law unto herself and did not respect any kind of boundaries as Pippa was going to find out the hard way.

CHAPTER 7

It started when soon after her arrival Pippa discovered furniture in her apartment would rearrange itself or even disappear altogether, and the only explanation was that someone was coming into the apartment at night when she was asleep, this worried her and made her feel insecure and somewhat violated, she had an idea who it was but she dare not confront her directly. So she decided to double lock her doors at night so even with a key no one could get n. Luckily Pippa had the sense to make an infantry of all the items in her apartment in the first few days of her arrival and had presented it to her employers to agree and sign so she was not worried about being accused of stealing because she recorded ever missing piece and dated it accordingly. The day after she locked her doors Lady Bee openly confronted Pippa on the matter complaining she could not access pipes apartment the night before. It was then that Pippa explained that her apartment was private and Lady Bee should regard it accordingly. She seemed impressed by Pippa's candour and agreed with her. However it later transpired that Lady Bee continued to snoop but covered her tracks more carefully during the day whilst Pippa was at work as there was no way to double lock the door from the outside. It was some time before Pippa realised this and although she felt helpless in stopping it, it would made her feel less guilty when the time came for her to leave at the end of her and Lissy's five year plan.

On the surface things ran like clockwork but underneath there was much contention and indecision relating to the organising of events. For instance the menu for the household was drawn up two weeks well in advance by Pippa and only signed off by Lady Bee who made very few changes to the family menu. However in the panic of an event she would change her mind continually almost (and sometimes) up to the day of the event which made things very difficult for Pippa who had to do the shopping for it. Sometimes it was a mad rush the very morning of the event Pippa would be driving into town between meals to get the ingredients for the meal that evening. Often this meant Pippa had no time to eat or drink herself. This was very frustrating as Pippa also had to do that cooking and preparation time was being wasted getting the ingredients most of which could have been bought or ordered in advance had decisions been made earlier.

Lady Bee didn't like waste which Pippa thought was an admirable quality however she turned out to be the biggest time and food waster in the house! For instance the menu was organised and signed off for two weeks so Pippa would shop accordingly making sure fresh stuff was available for each meal, however Lady Bee would arrive back from her outing with an unexpected basket full of fresh veg she had picked up from a market, a nice thought you might think but it meant the already bought veg would be wasted as there was only so much she could use for two people. It was never an option that Pippa could use the excess for herself or any of the other staff and naturally some could be frozen but Lady Bee would not eat frozen veg so inevitably some did go off and because she knew every leaf that came into the house there was no discreetly getting rid of the excess thus avoiding the chastening it was as if she was being set up for it. These were the nuances that confused Pippa she had trouble working people out at the best of times but this lady was a complete mystery, on the one hand she seemed as though she really wanted Pippa to succeed but on the other hand she seemed to sabotage her efforts. Her snooping led Pippa to think she did not trust her even though she would confide in her. Clearly she was not the full ticket. This was later confirmed in Pippa's mind because of events that transpired over the years she worked there.

An interesting thought occurred to Pippa here, and that was the fact that although Pippa's diet had not changed on entering service, she not only lost a healthy amount of weight but felt a lot fitter in herself, more focussed and alert. This was the result of her daily routine she decided one day whilst pondering the subject in front of the mirror before going to work. She knew she had guidance to help her perform her work from the Lord as she prayed daily and received inspiration but also the sheer size of the house had kept her fit as she walked the long halls and negotiated the stairs every day. She thought it would be an interesting experiment to see just how far she walked in a day, and so decided to download an app on her phone that calculated the distance she walked, she planned to take an average count over a week. This she did and was absolutely surprised with the results, she worked out that she had walked on average 22,493 steps daily, and concluded that there would never be any need to install a gym in a place like this! She wondered also if that was one of the reasons rich people stayed fit in spite of rich and plentiful foods and several courses to meals, as opposed to poorer people who had a larger proportion of obesity. Of course type of food and lifestyle played a bit part as did many other factors, but also did the size of property make a difference, she felt it had to as she was living proof.

It only took a **maximum** of 10 steps to walk from one room to the next in her little flat back home, here it would take 30-300 depending on your location in the rooms themselves. She wondered if anyone had ever made a study of that, then reprovingly thought to herself *"Would it be worth it if nobody really cared!"*

CHAPTER 8

"That's fine dear I will make the arrangements, I look forward to having you for the weekend, goodbye dear".   Lady Beatrice Elizabeth Buchannan sat back in her office chair, after hanging up the phone on her desk. She had spent the last hour or so talking to her daughter about a weekend visit she was planning. *"She has not given me much notice"* She complained inwardly.

Beatrice sighed as she pondered the conversation and the enormity of the demands that had been made, she fingered the notepad that she had jotted copious notes down on and instructions for the event on and flicked the pages. *"This is going to cost a pretty penny, but we cannot skimp and standards have to be kept, we cannot afford to show or let the children and guests know how bad finances are. Rupert is going to have a fit when I tell him, he is so up to his ears already with the expansion of the golf course"*. She drew her breath and continued in her thoughts trying to keep calm.

"There is little in the budget for lavish entertaining. Thank goodness for Pippa, she may be inexperienced but she learns quickly and costs a third of separate housekeeper and chef! By combining the two jobs I have saved £40,000 a year, by hiring her and Pippa's naivety meant she was none the wiser and unlikely to ask for any kind of pay rise." This made Beatrice smile, as she had thought herself very clever, and fortunate to have thought of this plan in the first place, her triumph was made complete when after a

couple of weeks working with Pippa she had proved very willing and pliable, she had got organisation and into the routine quickly and seemed unperturbed when new tasks were introduced into her schedule. For an untrained chef she had created some superb meals and shown she had no problem following a recipe. She was easy to teach too, she was eager and willing to please and clearly understated his abilities on her resume, she had proved she could turn her hand to very different tasks and do them well. The only thing that concerned Beatrice was her lack of social ability, she seemed shy when it came to dealing with clients, she had noticed this during wedding events and in spite of being invited to the festivities as the rest of the household attended, Pippa would retire after just a few minutes, not that it was part of her job but all the other staff enjoyed the free food and drink, was she shy, disinterested or anti –social? That was a subject Beatrice wou d probably approach with her at some point but for now it was neither here nor there.

Just when Pippa was beginning to relax and feel comfortable in her work and things seemed to be running quite smoothly. She was faced with a rather large challenge that threatened to knock her confidence right back to the beginning and see her return home a failure.

However a few days before the event Pippa arrived in her office that Monday morning to be greeted by a single post-it note stuck to her day book cover where lady Bee knew Pippa would see it immediately when she arrived at work in the morning.

As it was her custom to check the book before starting work Pippa paused to read its content and as expected it was from Lady Bee requesting Pippa to join her in the dining room at 10 am as she had something to discuss with her. At this point she had no idea what her ladyship had in mind to talk about but she knew it would become clear at the meeting and so she continued with her Monday chores keeping an eye on the time.

Monday was laundry day so one of her early morning chores was to strip the beds that had been slept in and change the sheets. The bed linen and any other large items were labelled and bagged up and put in plain sight in the utility room to be picked up by the contracted laundry service. Pippa collected the couple's personal washing and sorted it into piles of white's lights and darks before loading the washing machine with the whites going first.

Pippa busied herself until she saw it was about five to ten when she was emptying the dishwasher in the kitchen, next to the dining room. She quickly checked how she looked in the eye level oven window. And satisfied she was presentable she walked out of the open kitchen door into the stone floored hall, walked to the left a few steps and came to the Dining room back entrance door.

Pippa knocked and waited for a response, which she promptly received and so she turned the brass handle and entered the room. There were three doors in the dining room one adjoining the kitchen, which Pippa mostly and occasionally lady Bee used on a daily basis for setting up and clearing meals then there was the servants entrance which she now stood in front of, and a larger carved double wooden door that led into the main living room which the family and friends used. Pippa entered the room which she felt was quite imposing, it was large and square with a massive stone fireplace on her right, in the centre of the wall that also housed the double doors on the left of it, the cavernous aperture had no grate because it was not needed for logs, the estate forest supplied the sticks and logs needed to keep it stoked over winter and cool summer evenings. The gardener kept the log basket topped up daily. Pippa had already laid the fire previously so when she entered it was all prepared for a simple lighted taper to get it going as it always was kept in preparation for use.

A pair of high backed Queen Anne chairs faced the fire cn either side of the fireplace. Straight in front of her was the large dining table nestling one edge into the window recess.

A large heavy dark wood wall unit stretched along the left wall stopping just before the closed kitchen door, it housed all the silver for dining and bottles of the best spirits.

Lady Bee was sitting elegantly cross-legged on one of the matching dining chairs at the head of the table with papers spread over the table where she had been scribbling notes

. Pippa could not see details them from across the room and Lady Bee looked lost in her concentration and tiny amongst the ancient dark furniture which seemed to drown her in size. As Pippa approached the table Lady Bee looked up from her notes and over the top of her glassed and motioned Pippa to sit next to her. Without introduction to the subject Lady Bee launched right into the conversation. "A exis has confirmed her friends will be spending the weekend here and that means a dinner party on the Saturday evening so we have to discuss your menus and activities for the weekend" barely pausing for breath or to see Pippa's panicked and confused reaction, Lady Bee continued " Alexis and I have come up with some options that will be suitable for the event, we must have rosemary Lamb for the main course, and there will be fireworks after dinner Saturday evening with champagne and cocktails, and silver service ."   She continued to mutter as she referred to the notes and shuffled them around trying to find what she was looking and read from them the ideas she had jotted down. Pippa's brain had gone into overdrive and she could take no more in with the realisation of the enormity of the unexpected task required of her, thoughts where whirling around in her head and the sound of Lady bees voice became distant and inaudible. Then as if a light had been switched on in her head Lady T looked up again at Pippa who must have turned white because Lady Bee realised the poor girl looked overwhelmed and dumbfounded and she realised she had forgotten that this would be her first dinner party.

"So sorry Pippa I forgot you have never done this before and don't know the procedure, don't worry Ellen and I will talk you through it and I will be hiring silver service waiters for the night to help you."

Pippa tried to smile and respond but words were difficult in her confused state.

She managed to pull herself together to ask a couple of relevant questions about dates, times and order of events but could not take in all the details. She was relieved when Lady Bee handed her the wad of hand written notes for her to refer to, at least she would have that even if it was barely legible. She knew she would have a lot of questions over the next few days but right now she just wanted to catch her breath! She thanked Lady Bee and hurried out of the room and headed straight for her office to do just that she dropped the notes on the counter next to her day book. If ever she needed help from the Lord it was now, there was nothing pressing to do at that moment so she bounded up the stone stairs to her apartment and knelt by her bed in supplication, she felt sure this was one test she would fail and knew she may fail in some spectacular way that her job would be lost and she would embarrass herself and the family. She was not a trained chef and making meals for the family was one thing but formal silver service for visiting young entitled nobility?

Pippa was on her knees for about 20 minutes just pleading for help and guidance, and slowly she began to feel calmer and more peaceful and the things she had read in the scriptures passed through her mind and comforted her. She remembered that she was a child of God and He would help and guide her as she worked and give her inspiration when she needed it.

CHAPTER 9

"Pippa?" Lady Bee enquired

"What can I do for you?"

Pippa had just arrived in the large utility room that doubled as her office. It was a bright spring Tuesday morning. The sun shone brilliantly through the tall undressed sash windows and spread over the modern kitchen type surfaces and steel sink that lined the wall under the windows. The windows must have been at least ten feet tall above the surfaces. Everything in the room was modern, white and spotless unlike the rest of the manor which was quite dated.

Lady Bee had a folded piece of taupe linen in her hands which she offered up to Pippa, with the explanation "I hate the colour of this tablecloth, is it possible you could dye it for me?" Pippa took the cloth and moved over by the light of the tall sash windows to examine it better, and in her mind concluded the cloth must be new and unused, a woven linen, and hemmed around the edges. Large enough for a six foot table at least. Lady Bee had followed her expectantly and waited for the verdict.

"I don't see why not, what colour were you thinking of?"

"A nice royal blue I think"

"Why does that not surprise me?" Pippa mused inwardly

"I will get the dye when I do the shopping on Thursday and have it ready for you by Friday if that's ok"

"That will be fine there is no hurry, I will be in my office a l day today " Lady T informed her as she strode towards the door leaving the cloth with Pippa, when she got to the door she had a sudden thought, and turned again to face where Pippa was standing. "Will you need more cash for the dye?"

"No, Housekeeping will cover it." Pippa assured her

"Of course you are so good with the budget Rupert and I really appreciate that."

Pippa's chest swelled with pride at the complement, although it seemed like common sense to her to make the budget work. Being a single parent meant she had to stay within her own household budget because she had nothing to fall back on, mistakes would have caused serious crisis on such a small amount and she did not believe in getting into debt in fact she had a real fear of it and that made her thrifty and resourceful at making sure her figures balanced each month, it wasn't a choice it was a necessity. So to budget a large amount was no different to her and accurate records and receipts kept at all times. In fact it was one of her easiest jobs.

Almost as an afterthought "Oh and another thing before I go I would like to thank you for always looking smart at work, but not too smart as to out dress the quests." And with that Lady Bee left the room.

Confused Pippa thought to herself "Was that a compliment or a warning?" Pippa could not understand the meaning of that comment her only thought for her looks was to look smart and dress as if going to an office, no one had mentioned a dress code so it was just common sense to look smart but never even considered she might be in competition with guests! Either way she had once again inadvertently done the right thing in her Ladyships eyes!

Whilst musing on the almost pleasant exchange she looked closer at the cloth and wondered why Lady Bee hadn't just bought a blue cloth, perhaps it had been in a sale or something. Anyway no time to wonder about that she thought and she put the cloth over in the corner to await its new makeover, and drew the open diary that was on the surface to her. Her pen rested in the crevice of the pages and she lifted it and turned to the coming Friday and wrote 'Dye Cloth' onto the end of her list of jobs for that day.

Whilst work at the manor was not hard it did take meticulous organisation and managing, for this purpose Pippa had devised a series of tick sheets for each day of the week and a separate one for monthly tasks, like putting in orders for imported coffee. She recorded the dates she polished the brasses so that she wouldn't forget when they needed doing next. It was not just for her own benefit but when she was on holiday it was easy for someone to take over as they would know exactly what needed doing and when. Which is something she hadn't got and felt it might have been helpful when she started there. Menus were also prepared two weeks in advance. When creating these menus she often wondered what it was like in the old days of the house. She had read period fiction and watched period dramas on TV about the lives of the army maids and cooks and butlers and such in Victorian times and she wondered what they would think of it all now, the whole house being run by just one chief cook and bottle washer so to speak. So much had changed since then.

Thursday came and she drove the company car to the local town around 1 pm. She went directly to the reserved parking area used by manor staff. Thursdays was market day so parking would be a nightmare had it not been for the reserved spaces. Working at the manor afforded some privileges and easy parking was a particular one Pippa enjoyed. Not having to search for a space made her job so much easier. She worked through her usual list of stores and stalls, (some of which recognised the basket and to the manor it belonged and she was treated with great respect by the merchants and regular shop staff) with basket and list in hand she completed the purchases on her list. Lady T did not like carrier bags and so Pippa was obliged to use the wicker basket provided for the purpose, the only trouble was that it didn't hold much so she brought cardboard boxes with her and had them on the back seat of the car and she would periodically return to the car and offload the basket into the boxes. After about the third trip this day she decided the best place to find a dye might be the local Boyes store as she was sure she had seen some there on a previous visit. So she strode to the opposite end of the small main road of shops to where Boyes was situated and went in to browse as much as anything else. She wandered up and down the aisles making a mental note of where things of interest to her were especially in the craft section which she loved. She found a lovely stamp of a robin on a branch which she fancied would make lovely handmade cards and so she picked it up longingly and studied the intricate design. " But when would I have time?" she chided herself, and returned it to the shelf, and then decided to stop messing about and just go and get the item she came in for!

There was quite selection of blue colour dyes on the shelf but Pippa knew Lady Bee would not settle for less than a royal blue label at whatever the cost, and as expected it was not the cheapest either. Pippa aimed to please and followed instructions to the letter wherever possible and this was no exception and so the item was duly purchased and hauled back to the manor with all the rest of the shopping. Pippa took it to her apartment that evening to read the instructions closely so she would know what to do the next day as she knew it was a long process and would need to be acted on early in the day.

Friday (Fry-Dye as she had dubbed it in her journal the night before) arrived and just for extra confidence she appealed to the Lord in her morning prayers for success in her new endeavour as she had not dyed anything before and this fabric was not hers and for all she knew it was of some value to Lady T. So after laying out the breakfast things in the morning room she came back to the utility room and double checked the instructions and followed them to the letter, adding the exact quantity of dye and set the programme exactly as directed on the packet and within trepidation she set the machine in motion. She had plenty of other chores to see to but she kept detouring to check the cycle was operating correctly fully expecting something to go amiss. When the machine finally finished its cycle Pippa couldn't wait to see what had happened and she pulled the cloth out of the barrel to examine it. She spread it out and looked for any flaws (although she did not have a clue what she would do if there were any) and with a satisfied sigh of relief she saw that there were none and it had come out a lovely shade of blue fit for the Lady Bee and all that remained was to dry it and iron it and by mid- afternoon she had done just that. With an air of competence and gratitude for a well- executed task Pippa went to find Lady Bee whom she knew to be in her office. She gently knocked on the door and was invited in, lady Bee looked up from her work and instantly recognised the tablecloth and its fine new colour. "Is that the cloth? She asked rhetorically.

Pippa beamed with pride in response to the compliment.

"It looks so different, thank you Pippa I knew I could count on you" and Lady Bee took the cloth from Pippa's hand and opened it out to admire it and laid it on an adjoining table to Lady Bees desk. Pippa thought it was fit to adorn any table and Lady Bee commented "That looks quite handsome now." She said before refolding it and handing it back to Pippa.

"Glad you like it, are you ready for your afternoon tea and biscuits?"

"Yes I think it's time for a break in about ten minutes

"Ok ten minutes it is"   Pippa returned to the utility room and placed the cloth in the linen cupboard (with a great feeling of satisfaction) along with all the rows of mainly white other household linen to wait to be used in the near future.

CHAPTER 10

A few days later Lady Bee announced that after breakfast she was going to attempt to decorate the nursery room in the north wing where traditionally the five small children's rooms and nannies room were located. And she would take afternoon tea in there that afternoon. The day went smoothly and it came time for afternoon tea and Pippa prepared the usual tray consisting of small pink floral china teapot with matching china cup, saucer, milk jug, sugar bowl and side-plate, set on a white cotton and lace doily. The plate having a selection of three hand baked biscuits. As the children's rooms were on the other side of the house to the utility room it was important that the hot water was the last task done before quickly walking the distance of the halls, up the central stairs and left down the west wing hall to the last of the six doors she knew to be the nursery.

Standing in front of the door and balancing the tray in her left hand she knocked on the door before entering, knowing she was expected now at 3pm which was the usual afternoon tea time. Just inside there were a couple of steps down into the room which she carefully descended and glanced around the room to locate her ladyship. The room was light and airy, and mainly cream and white, and smelt of emulsion paint and the decorating trappings were strewn around the room. Her attention was quickly directed at Lady Bee who was kneeling by the window just finishing a patch of cream wall under it. She turned and slowly got up and with a clear sigh of relief. "Just what I need" she announced gratefully "What do you think Pippa, I thought neutral so it does not matter what sex the baby is?"

Pippa found a paint splattered dust covered chest of drawers and set the tray down on it while Lady Bee began to pour her tea.

"Who's pregnant?"

"Nobody yet but my girls are of that age I doubt it will be long, and I am looking forward to babysitting duties."

"Ah well I think neutral is very sensible in that case, and you have done a grand job." She observed as she turned a full 360 degree circle surveying the DIY scene. What caught her eye as she turned quite shocked her as she recognised the lovely royal blue table cloth draped over a pine wardrobe also covered in cream paint splatter?

It was lucky Lady Bee was distracted at that very moment because Pippa s first reaction was to challenge her about it but she managed to bite her tongue and turn her face back towards the door and headed towards it trying not to explode at Lady Bee's total disregard for her work with the table cloth. "I'll be down in plenty of time for tea." Lady Bee called after her as she closed the door behind her By the time she reached the utility room she had begun to see the funny side and calm down after all not only had Lady Bee paid for the dye etc. but she had in effect paid for Pippa's time and for what!? Obviously Lady Bee had not worked out the cost effectiveness of the whole thing and Pippa just had to giggle to herself about the sheer stupidity and wastefulness. It's not just how the other half live she concluded but how they think and she chuckled again.

"I should write that down somewhere it sounds like a COMEDY ROUTINE!"

CHAPTER 11

It was generally the case that Pippa's holidays were planned to coincide with the families holidays which had worked out quite well over the years she was there. On occasion she would be invited to an event with the family such as Christmas pantomimes, Agricultural shows and the like. At first Pippa though this might be one of the perks of the job but she soon discovered this was not the case and she found out the hard way again, the first being the local agricultural show.

It was during one of her usual morning meetings in the dining room with her ladyship that Lady Bee brought up the upcoming agricultural show which was only a fortnight away

"Would you like to go to the agricultural show on the 21st (it was then the 8th of August)," I never go to these things anymore I find them tedious". Lady Bee declared but "Rupert loves them and he is quite happy to take you if you like, he will be in the VIP area so you would have to amuse yourself for the day." she continued.

"I will invite a friend and we can meet up there I enjoy that sort of thing and I can get some photos of the horses to paint later" She was thinking out loud again.

Lady Bee made a mental note. *"So she paints too, I wonder what else she does and how can I tap that resource?"*

Pippa made a quick note in her pad of the date and details before looking at Lady Bee in anticipation for her next instruction.

"Well that is sorted" Lady Bee affirmed as she looked back down at her list, ticked next to the word 'Show' and moved her pen down the list to find the next subject to discuss on her agenda for the day which included the upcoming fortnights menu, in anticipation Pippa had picked up the rough copy of the menu she had planned and they discussed a few small changes to that.

It was not long before the day of the show arrived and Pippa was ready and waiting in her office to be notified of Lord Bee's departure, she was absentmindedly looking out of the window when a young woman sporting a long sleek pony tail of dark hair, (she was one of the office staff Pippa rarely had contact with) entered the room and confidently announced Lord Bee was waiting in the car at the front of the house for Pippa. She grabbed her shoulder bag from the surface and thanked the girl and headed off to where Lord Bee was waiting in his banged up old Land-rover.

Lord Bee was a man of few words or so it seemed as he made very little conversation on the drive to the showground, they were in the car for twenty to thirty minutes and other than arranging a time to meet up to come home he seemed disinterested in conversation which suited Pippa as she did not know what to talk about anyway!

They arrived at the grounds and were ushered to parking spaces, then they walked towards the crowds waiting in line at the turnstiles. One of which was heaving and the other almost empty and of course that one was the VIP entrance, which Lord Bee strode confidently towards, gesturing Pippa towards the other gate to take her turn with 'the others' and to pay for her own ticket! He on the other hand flashed his VIP card and waltzed straight through the barrier unimpeded. And there he left her alone to wait with the commoners! In Pippa's mind she had expected to enter the grounds together then split up but not just be abandoned at the entrance, perhaps she expected too much but she was very disgruntled about the dismissive treatment. She had invited a friend to meet up with but they had cancelled before she left that morning, so Pippa was alone for the whole day, so she wandered about and watched a dog training display which whiled away an hour, she watched bee keeping lectures and sampled some of the hand- made pies and cakes. She watched the magnificent dressage competition and admired the elegance of the horses' precision steps and appearance. She busied herself taking photographs of the performing animals and trainers. She watched as the shire horses were meticulously groomed and harnessed to wagons and of course took photos, she even found a cute little foal tied to a horse box patiently waiting for its mother to return from her work, she just had to get a picture of that!

The place was bustling with onlookers made up of families out for the day and friends of the contestants cheering them on. It was a warm sunny day and everyone seemed happy to be there and finally not long before she was to head back to the car she decided she wanted an ice-cream to end the day with which is exactly what she did, and finding the nearest van she ordered a large waffle 99 with hand- made vanilla ice cream, and while enjoying this lavish treat, a thought occurred to her, and she felt she was being rather naughty, *"I will put the cost of my ticket on the housekeeping expenses"* and looking at her ticket which she had pulled out of her pocket of her jeans, yes that will make a good receipt, she knew she would have to account for the purchase but she saved them a lot of money from month to month so they would probably not even notice. She smiled cheekily and slipped the ticket back in her pocket and headed for the designated meeting point still smugly eating her treat.

Most of her personal holidays were spent at home with her family, catching up and organising her finances around the cost of her flat. Occasionally her and Lissy would attend church conferences together or had day trips to the seaside all of which she loved. The most exciting and most eventful holiday was the one to France, on a scouting expedition for the much dreamed of Bed and Breakfast property in 2004

CHAPTER 12

Pippa had thought it wise not to inform anyone at the manor her five year plan, not only because she was unsure it would come to pass but she knew if it were known she may not have even been accepted for the post, it would change the working dynamic that she was up to now enjoying. She was quite clear in her mind that although she had some loyalty to her employers, to give good service and do her work well, they did not own her nor would they have any loyalty should their circumstances change that they had no need of her that she would be discarded without a second thought. That is not to say that she was rigid in her execution of her work, quite the opposite she was flexible and willing to accommodate any task needed. Including staying up late one weekday evening just to help a film crew who had been filming a period drama with their work, she had to run from room to room switching lights on and off when required so they could film evening scenes outside the manor with lights on in certain rooms.

The job was very important to Pippa but not so important that she would allow her dignity to be compromised in any way as in the incident with the silver service dinner four years ago and more since. She would not work on Sundays as it was the Lords day. She did not know if they could sack her for it or make life difficult for her but she was prepared to take that consequence, she was lucky in that it gained her even more respect in the end.

Meanwhile as time went on and she was entering the fifth year of employment in 2005, it soon became apparent that her and Lissy had done exceptionally well in savings for their venture that they did not have long to go before they could actually start the ball rolling. The rent from their combined English properties would also keep them afloat whilst they built up a customer base. They had decided that would be better than simply selling up and they could always do that at a later date if necessary. They had considered somewhere in England and Ireland but prices were prohibitive and Irelands inclement weather would have proved problematic for several reasons, including the fact they wanted to include themed holidays for painting and photography, and as lovely as the scenery was there it was often too damp to accommodate classes of artists outdoors. So they had decided to have a holiday in France as property seemed much cheaper there and fares cheap enough for family to visit quite often via the ferry. Lissy could speak fluent French and had taught Pippa a little bit in preparation for the visit which had calmed Pippa's anxiety, assuring her she would pick it up much easier once they were there. The weather there was also a bonus as winters were short.

Pippa had never been out of the country before and this was going to be a very new experience for her, she never would have dared go somewhere alone much less a foreign country so her excitement was intertwined with anxiety but it did not diminish it. The days before the trip seemed to drag and she found it hard to think of anything else.

CHAPTER 13

One evening as she laid in bed staring at the ceiling as the summer light began to fade, she began to compare her life no to what it had been years ago. How she had been in the depths of despair, in so much pain mentally and physically that she was unable to function at times, and on the brink of ending it altogether, how close she had come to death, she shivered at the thought that she may have succeeded and missed all these wonderful experiences. She also thought of the times her health had failed and she had come close to death during her recovery. She considered it a miracle she was even alive at this time let alone doing so well. She did not feel her life was particularly special in the overall plan of the universe, to have been blessed with these miracles but she knew that finding and living the gospel standards would mean that she and her children were taught integrity and good standards that helped them grow as people, to Love the

Lord and be kind to others so that who knows what they and their children may be (or achieve) in the future, they would good citizens at least. She knew she would never again feel abandoned by God. Looking at the world in general it seemed to Pippa quite lacking in good moral standards and governments seemed determined to undermine good honest family values. "Pippa!" she chided herself for letting her mind wander so much, as she noticed the room was almost enveloped in the dark of night, reluctantly she rolled over determined not to think along these lines anymore and to try and get some sleep. *"Only two sleeps and she would be off on a new adventure".* She thought as she smiled smugly to herself and drifted into a more pleasant peaceful little world of sleep. "It's today!" Pippa exclaimed as she threw off the bedclothes and launched herself out of bed, and turned the alarm off. She knelt beside the bed and said a quick prayer of grateful thanks for this lovely opportunity ahead of her. Hurriedly she gathered her clothes and headed for the shower where she could not help but sing some of her favourite songs while she showered and got dressed. The morning sun beamed through the windows in both rooms and usually she would awake on summer mornings and listen to the cacophony of birdsong that drifted in through her open windows before the alarm went off for work. Today was different she was up early so the symphony had only just begun and today she was adding her voice in their chorus. They did not seem to mind her rough off key notes and continued to sing along with her or so it seemed to her!

CHAPTER 14

Never having been on a boat before was a daunting thought but Pippa was up for the new experience and was determined to savour every new experience. She fully expected to feel sea sick but was pleasantly surprised at the end of the journey that she had not felt sick in the least, although the movement of the boat did disorientate her at times. She enjoyed wandering through the decks and chatting with Lissy and looking out over the ocean. However bedtime was a different story, she was unable to sleep and the ideas of the many ways disaster could strike kept her from relaxing, thoughts of whether she could swim to shore if they sank and every ship disaster movie she had seen replayed in her head! No matter how she told herself she was being unreasonable she could not block the thoughts. She also became acutely aware of the ships sounds and movements, she felt herself lifting with her bunk over every wave and almost held her breath as everything seemed to her to stop for a second or two at the top before she felt the stomach churning fall seemingly through space and land with a thump.

After a very long tense night she was so relieved when the alarm went off and she could get up! When she told Lissy of her nightmarish experience all Lissy could do was laugh heartily at her friend, whilst she tried to also comfort her and reassure her she simply could not help herself. "Seriously Pippa, this ferry goes to and from France every other day, I doubt it will sucdenly sink on your first trip!" Lissy had to stop talking and wipe away her tears and take a breath between gaffaws, Pippa had already seen the funny side and finally broke into laughing herself more because Lissy's laughter was infectious than feeling reassured but once she began laughing too all the tension and fear just melted away in a fit of merriment.

Lissy found it amusing to watch Pippa's awed expression, and excitement, as the new sights and experiences hit her like a kid at the fair for the first time. Over the next few days there were many such things to lighten her face and Lissy appreciated being able to experience them with her it was catching too.

Lissy and Pippa decided to drive directly to their accommodation in the little town of Renaze as it was a fair distance from the docks they had landed at about 10 am that morning. By the time they managed to disembark, negotiated customs and found their way out onto the open road it was almost noon. They had packed a lunch in anticipation so they had no need to find somewhere to eat. They planned to arrive in Renaze about 2.30 pm if all went well, then settle in, freshen up, orientate themselves by going for a walk, then come back and freshen up before dinner about 7pm. After Dinner another walk around the town still getting a little more orientated seemed like a good plan.

So Lissy concentrated on getting into the flow of traffic and onto the right road that led to Renaze. At the same time getting used to being on the other side of the road. The town seemed very little different from any towns Pippa had seen in England apart from the signs were in French of course. It did seem a little cleaner and less dense if that was the right word to describe it.

As the buildings seemed to get sparser and the scenery became more green and open, Pippa looked around with awe. "Wow, so much space around here the view goes on forever." She announced her thought out loud without realising she had.

"The roads are so straight too, and the land is flat for miles. Straight roads are a novelty at first but can bore you to sleep after a while especially as there is so little traffic." Chuckled Lissy.

Practical as ever Pippa said ruefully "It would not do to break down on these long deserted roads, remind me to put together some emergency supplies for our travelling. I have not even seen a dwelling for the past 15 minutes."

"It is not that bad we do have a reasonable phone signal."

"Just the same if it is only garage numbers and food I would feel better." Pippa persisted.

"Ok, I will leave that to you to sort out if it makes you feel better."

"How do people sort out their shopping and stuff way out here?"

"Well farmers are quite self- sufficient, as you would expect and they often supply local shops, there are very few jobs so everyone grows their own food, bake their own bread. They make planned trips together for other less urgent supplies and in some areas you can get stuff delivered or they get together and share the cost of a trip. It takes more organising and there is less waste to say the least and a good sense of community. Having said that with people coming into the country and buying property like us there is a boom in building anc DIY work, and a better network growing culture of tourism because like us we will be providing accommodation we will never be stuck for DIY people for our place. I have found in the rural areas the French have a philosophy of a kind they work to live, and when they have enough for their needs they see no reason to continue working, they do not live for work as we do. You often find shops only open half days especially fresh food and bakery, they make enough for their needs for the day then simply close, go home and enjoy the rest of the day!"

The few gardens Pippa had seen she now realised had few pretty flowers in them but a lot of green, she realised now that was because growing food was far more practical than flowers, not that she had not seen any colour it had just been few and far between, In England gardens would be a full blaze of colour and scents by now.

"I love this place already." Pippa declared, she sighed and relaxed back into her seat to watch the moving countryside as it whizzed past her window and just breathed it all in through her open window. She savoured the feeling and the wind as it caressed and blew her hair into strange alien forms around her face.

They had not been long out of the town and on the country roads Lissy pulled over on the deserted road and picked up her mobile phone and found the name Rhonda and clicked on it and within seconds a familiar woman's voice answered.

"Bonjour Lissy. " Came the female voice on the other end "Where are you?"

"Bonjour Rhonda, we are in France and driving straight to yours, we will be with you in about two hours, maybe less."

"I can't believe you are really here, I have gathered some information on properties round about for you to look at and can't wait to show you."

"We can do all of that tomorrow so we can just catch up this evening and you and Pippa can get to know each other too."

"Bonjour Pippa." Rhonda shouted

"Bonjour Rhonda, I look forward to meeting you."

"Me too I shall have your rooms ready when you arrive and the evening meal will be 7 until 9 o'clock. That will give us plenty of time to chat Charles can wait on me for a change, see you both soon, au revoir for now."

The call ended and the girls relaxed and began to appreciate lovely scenery and open space as it passed them by. The roads being unusually quiet compared to English roads and straighter, the road seemed to disappear into the distance with very few landmarks to break it up. They seemed very alone on that road which made Pippa question the location for a business and she turned to Lissy and said, "How will people find us out here and is it a bit far from anywhere for tourists?"

"We are not looking at the tourist market we will be more niche, we are targeting artists and photographers, we, will be offering workshops and will be quite self-contained. We will also be offering cookery and growing workshops which will help us sustain a kitchen garden."

"Will we really be able to afford such a large property with land?"

"Easily, you will not believe the prices here and it is why Brits come here, Rhonda has been pestering me for a long time to come and have a look, ever since I met her, oooh, must be three years or more ago when she came home to visit family and friends, one of which was my employer at the time."

"How will we attract custom from way out in the sticks?"

"Word of mouth initially, but they still have internet here and many travel agents are looking for out of the way places and unusual destinations. Activity holidays are all the rage now so it will not be too difficult and like all new businesses it takes time to build a reputation and customer base. We will be fine." Lissy reassured her.

Pippa sat back and pondered all of this in her mind, she had been dreaming of this for so long and here they were actually looking at properties and making plans. She knew the secret to being successful was diversity, Art workshops, cooking and growing food, not to mention the sale of artists materials and possibly a gallery of her own and customers work, gave them a good chance of success. Making connections through mutual friends was also essential and Rhonda was one of many who would be happy to help and vice versa. Pippa knew plenty of artist friends that would jump at the chance of a free holiday in return for teaching workshops in the summer. It would be hard work to begin with just the two of them but once income was being generated there would be money to hire staff to help and that would be when Pippa would have time to work on her own art. That was the general idea anyway.

As she stared at the dilapidated rows of stables, a dark memory flitted across her mind, a distant memory that was more like a bad dream than a memory now, or maybe a scene in a play she saw, or chapter of a book she read. Deep down though she knew it was real. Pippa was used to these flashbacks and was able to departmentalise.

<h1 style="text-align:center">CHAPTER 15</h1>

Pippa stood on the grassy verge in the black envelope of night. Shivering with cold and fear. Scantily dressed as she had escaped in a hurry not thinking of anything else but getting away.

She patted the muzzle of one of the ponies who's heads were leaning over the fence in apprehensive curiosity, she had stopped running and had chosen to stop there for breath and to engage with these creatures, the only living things for miles it seemed., She watched as she caressed them as their breath created steam clouds that were clearly discernible despite the darkness.

As her hands passed over the rough winter coat of its neck, she felt the warmth of its body seeping into her hand, and she thought how this may be the the last piece of comfort she may ever feel again in her life, there was nothing behind her and it seemed to her there was nothing in front of her physically, mentally or even emotionally, this was it.

The ebony skies and blackened view around her seemed to reflect what was inside of her, a chasm of darkness she could not see an end of. Clothed in only a summer dress and wrap coat, and sandals (the only clothes she possessed since leaving home 3 months earlier), it began snowing, and the flakes floated down and alighted on the faces of girl and pony alike, they tickled her eyelashes and made her blink, and the flakes melted into her warm tears and ran down her face.

The two creatures in front of her were her only comfort standing there, and she began to talk in low whispers and pour out her broken heart to them. They did not judge as she explained the mistakes that had led her to the man who was so cruel to her. How he had taken her tender heart and tender years and twisted them until they were broken and without hope. How there was no pit deeper or darker than the one she had dug for herself and now felt she could not escape. The ponies ears twitched as they listened to her silently, and the sound of their regular breathing seemed to calm her. But nothing could stop her wondering what now? She had escaped the immediate threat but to where, to whom would she go? She could think of no-one at all that would want her especially now.

The hopelessness of her situation again overwhelmed her already delicate senses and she began to sob uncontrollably and her entire body shook and she thought she would feint as her strength simply dissipated and it was all she could do to stay on her feet. She could not think in any other way than blackness and hopelessness, it permeated her very being. The now, the pain, the confusion, the emptiness inside. So many questions Why her? What now? What was the point? And so many more that just could not be answered. She thought about the gaily lighted windows she had passed before ending up on this long lonely road, of the people inside preparing to celebrate, families around the fire, laughing and interacting, and how she was on the outside of everything, they did not even know of her existence, nobody did even at that moment her abuser lay in a drunken stupor would not know of her existence she had no control over anything. So what if she just slipped out of existence………..

Just then a car pulled up alongside the verge she had crossed to get to the ponies, up until then she had not been aware of any other vehicles. A mans voice broke the silence through the open passenger window "you Ok? You need a lift somewhere?"

She breathed in her tears and her heart began to pound, this was not the notice she craved for but it was all that had been offered and for a fleeting moment she really desperately wanted to accept the offer. All sorts of senarios flashed through her mind, this could be her salvation and her escape and someone to help but on the other hand was it possible to jump out of one fire into another, and it seemed like an age she was riveted to the spot with all of this swirling around her head until finally she involuntarily blurted out "No thanks , I am waiting for someone."

Clearly unconvinced the driver rolled up his window and went on his way and as she watched his tail lights disappear into the distance she wondered if she had just let her only chance get away or had she had a narrow escape and she concluded she would never know now. Would anything have been as bad as she was suffering now anyway? These thoughts now tore at her mind on top of everything else now. In silence again her heart beat began to slow as she turned back to the patiently waiting ponies, they had been enjoying her company and touch. In all the turmoil of her mental anguish she had forgotten her physical pain and now her fresh injuries and now they began to ache and smart especially her jaw and left eye which was probably black and she realised was probably visable, in the car headlights a moment ago, no wonder the man looked unconvinced!

Whilst all this was going on the snow had silently covered everything around and the darkness was no longer absolute. One of the ponies shook his head and main vigorously spraying a blanket of snow out and away from itself. Soon it would be light and the world would be waking up and she realised that she would be clearly seen and suddenly she felt exposed and she felt like a rabbit caught in the headlights, finding a policeman to ask for help was something she had tried befcre and not been taken seriously, she was simply told to find somewhere to go or go home as there was nothing they could do. She had no choice she had to go back or stand there for all to see, and nowhere to hide. She had to go back…………

CHAPTER 16

"You ok?" These words broke the scene before her eyes and she blinked as the 'visionary spell' seemed to break and she was jogged back into the present by the need to respond. "Yeh, just drinking it all in." She lied. It had played out in seconds in reality but she felt she had been back there for hours and time had slowed down inside her mind. The rest of the viewings went without incident until finally they made the decision (whilst enjoying the cuisine at the B&B each evening) which property best suited their needs. It was then up to Lissy to go over the details with the Noteier and translate to Pippa what was happening and where to sign.

Pippa was able to find time to paint some of the lovely rustic scenes she came across as they travelled including a farm in Armeille.

Pippa drew a little attention when she painted at times and not least the owner of the farm she painted, she seemed to creep up behind Pippa and stand for some time watching her paint before making her presence known by clearing her throat. This made Pippa jump a little as she was oblivious to her presence.

Pippa greeted her in French and soon they were chattering in broken English and French but somehow with gestures and elementary French they seemed to be able to communicate quite well. They exchanged first names and it turned out Bianca (the ladies name) had lived at the farm all her life and were self- sufficient it appeared. Bianca loved the painting Pippa was doing (but not enough to offer to buy it Pippa noted).

When the conversation dried up, they animated their goodbyes and Bianca left Pippa to go back to her painting which by now was almost done, suddenly she had an impulse that she must sketch her because she seemed to have come from a different era as her attire was that of an 18th century peasant, was this national costume? She had not noticed it before as she had to focus on finding the right words to communicate with this stranger. Had things changed so little over the years in rural areas! Was she at all real? Pippa had begun to question the whole encounter, how did she not see her coming? Was her concentration on the farm affecting her concept of reality? Looking back on the event she wondered as it was such a strange encounter and it played on her mind for a long time to come. When she relayed her experience and showed Lissy and Rhonda the sketch of the woman they could hardly believe it either, Rhonda especially asserted that in all her years living in the rea she had never come across anyone dressed in that fashion!

CHAPTER 17

After handing in her notice Pippa had been prepared and excited to work the required months' notice, knowing she had a new life to look forward to, and although she expected the relationships in the house to cool and change during that time. Nothing prepared her for the complete change in attitude towards her and her work as up until then Lady Bee had sung her praises and was entirely happy with her work, she often commented on how Pippa had brought the house to life again and her organisation skills were spot on.

It began with Lady Bee following her around as he went about her usual tasks and threatening Pippa at every opportunity.

"You had better not be going to another job, I won't stand for it I will make sure you never work again." Pippa believed her too. She also wondered if somehow she knew what she had planned but how could she?

"I am homesick and feel isolated that's all it is I just want to go home." Pippa protested defensively.

"That better be the reason." Lady Bee hissed

Pippa desperately bit her tongue, not because she was afraid Lady Bee would make good her threat because she knew she would win any legal battle, but simply that she still to this day could not handle confrontation and she was scared she would say something that would escalate the already uncomfortable situation. *"Just see it through to the end of the notice."* she kept telling herself.

Homesickness was only partly true as she and Lissy had finally saved enough to buy their own guest house and Pippa also wanted spend some time at home before entering a new phase of her life. Pippa was glad she had not stated her entire reasons for leaving on her formal notice. Who knows what her reaction would have been to that!

Pippa was perplexed and confused as what was it to Lady Bee if she wanted to move to a different job? What difference would it make to her other than having to hire someone else which may have been inconvenient but was the natural way of the work place? After all she had done her job well whilst she was there but had never given the impression it was going to be there indefinitely most people in most jobs moved on for whatever reason. To Pippa it was just a job. Yes she was expecting Lady Bee to be disappointed with her choice but not to the extent she would turn nasty and that is exactly what was happening. Pippa felt unsafe for the first time since moving in 5 years ago, and even when Lady T would visit her apartments during the night Pippa had not felt in any danger as she realised Lady

Bee was simply eccentric and perhaps not sure of boundaries in her own home.

Meanwhile each day became more tense and the threats more frequent and Pippa was not quite sure how to handle it. Lady Bee was not about to let her go without making her feelings known. She was not just disappointed but quite possessive as though Pippa was stealing her prize horse! It made her so uncomfortable and she dreaded going in each day, but hey she only had to see it through only another two weeks to go. *"Just bite your tongue for another couple of weeks Pip for goodness sake and you will be free."*

It all came to a head about two weeks into her notice when as previously planned Lady Bee had visitors for a few days, another Lord and Lady, which Pippa was looking forward to and although she did not know these friends of Lady Bee she was hoping their visit would take her mind off Pippa's departure.

Whilst discussing the week's events and menus Pippa had expressed her slight change of routine to accommodate the visitors and Pippa's extra work load one of which was that she would leave the usual Mondays washing until Wednesday unless there was something in particular Lady Bee needed during that time.

"I really just want to redistribute the work that's all as Wednesdays were usually a slow day so the washing could be done then, that way I won't be rushing about on Monday and it's only a couple of days difference." she explained.

"I want you to do it on Monday!" Lady Bee demanded

"Why must it be done on Monday when I am doing extra work unless you want to wear something in particular that is in the wash, is there?"

"No I just want it done."

Thinking she was being petulant Pippa tried to reassure Lady Bee that she was not avoiding doing the work she was just managing her time more productively. However it seemed Lady Bee was just exercising her authority over Pippa and that was when she realised Lady Bee was being an outright bully and that put her back up.

"Look, Lady Bee have a little faith in me I am here to take the pressure off you so you can enjoy your time with your friends, so just leave things to me they will get done, and go and enjoy your time together, and I will start on lunch in ten minutes."

Lady Bee looked less than happy but she couldn't think of a reply and turned on her heals and stormed off into the sitting room where her guests were enjoying the tea Pippa had taken in earlier.

Pippa thought that was the end of the incident. Oh boy was she wrong.

The rest of Monday passed without incident and Pippa happily worked longer than her normal hours as the extra housework, meals, and drinks picnic lunches as well as preparing the house for a wedding later in the week took a little longer than usual but that was nature of the job so to speak and was really no big deal.

So come Tuesday morning after bringing in the milk and papers from the back doorstep, and delivering the newspapers to the offices of Lord Bee along with a morning coffee, Pippa headed for the utility room where she found several shirts half soaked in the sink no doubt an attempt by Lady Bee to force Pippa to do the washing after all as she had demanded, as though she had been watching for her Lady Bee appeared in the room behind her watching for Pippa's reaction to what she had done. Pippa was not about to be bullied even by a titled person, it was obvious she was being tested and pushed into a confrontation. And so in an effort to avoid it Pippa in a light-hearted way said "You had an accident?"

"No." Lady Bee snapped back at her

Pippa feigned surprise, "Ok then well I hope you will finish that washing as I told you I don't have time till Wednesday.' she said as she pulled down her workbook off the shelve and turned to the page where she had listed Tuesdays jobs and began to read hoping Lady Bee would give up on her quest.   She was not prepared for the sudden verbal abuse that followed and the high pitch of her voice that carried the length and breadth of the manor and consequently to the ears of the visiting dignitaries. Suspecting this was Lady Bee's design to assert her authority in front of her friends, and expecting Pippa to also raise her voice and join in the display. She also placed herself right in front of Pippa threateningly causing her to step back against the door of the linen room which was closed so she could back away no further. Pippa felt trapped and intimidated and she began to flash back. To being pinned against a wall with a knife at her throat..........

CHAPTER 18

Waking up in a hospital bed was the last thing she wanted or expected and she was quite angry with the doctors and nurses around her and this did not improve her state of mind. Why on earth would they bother to save her? Now she had the humiliation of failure to add to her overwhelmed senses, now she would have to explain herself to her mum whom she thought would be very angry with her. To top that her assigned psychologist was convinced she had been rejected by a love interest and avoided dealing with the bullying issues! That experience compounded her feelings of not belonging, being odd, subnormal, strange even.

Surprisingly her mum was not angry and tried to understand but Pippa felt even she could not explain the turmoil and pain she felt her mum did watch her like a hawk after that and then she felt like a prisoner on top of everything else. By this time her feelings had become strangely numb and felt she was simply going through the motions of living, aimless and friendless now she had changed schools the bullying had stopped but she was not able to make any friends and so again felt ostracised and invisible, and somehow lacking in that she did not have a boyfriend like all the other girls, all she could think of was finding an escape from her life and someone to care for her and love her even, was that the solution? Finding a boyfriend? Although, it took her many years to discover what love really was as her only experience up until then had been comic strip stories of boys and girls finding love and walking hand in hand into the sunset to live happily ever after! But who could ever love her?

Certainly she could think of no boy in her class that would give her a second look. That was when she began to deceive her family in order to attend pubs and clubs during the school day hoping to find someone that way. It nobody missed her at school once again she was adept at being invisible. She found a man 26 years old eager to have sex with a willing minor. She ran away from home and landed on his doorstep which was probably the last thing he expected or wanted. It goes without saying what she found was anything but love and ended up married to an older man whom she was to discover was an alcoholic and very abusive. So no happy ending there! Her life then became one long round of physical and mental abuse which went on for nearly 5 years and at first she was convinced she deserved it because she had no idea how to keep house or be a wife, but gradually even she wised up and on her 3rd escape attempt to a woman's refuge home managed to succeed at long last. Her first two attempts failing as conditions in the homes were just as intimidating as the situation she was trying to escape. To describe these years would disturb any sane mind and many would find it unbelievable that it could have occurred in what we feel is a civilised country such as ours. It is also a whole other story.

However one particular incident has to be touched on because it is pivotal to the comparative nature of the 'before and after' of her remarkable story of pain, betrayal, bitterness to forgiveness, hope and success.

Pippa could not remember what sparked the violence of that afternoon but she knew it would have been some minor irritation to her husband that he escalated in his mind that he felt he had to punish her. She was heavily pregnant with her third child and her two older ones were upstairs in bed asleep or so she hoped. She already ached with bruises from the last beating on her arms and shoulders where she had curled up in a ball to protect the unborn child inside her, his fists only gairing access to her back arms and legs.

Her husband was bad tempered at the best of times but he was much worse when he was 'drying out' after binge drinking for several days at a time. So this situation was no surprise and she had learned there was no appeasing him and she simply had to weather the beatings as she had so many times before, however this time they had somehow ended up in the narrow hallway, the door facing the stairs up to the second floor of the house, he had her back pinned to the narrow hallway wall where the light switch dug into her shoulders, she was facing the front door, his left arm across her chest and a kitchen knife at her throat and his face distorted in anger, and she could clearly see the veins pulsing in his neck as his face was right in hers and he spat profanities at her and threatened her life. In spite of fearing for her own and her unborn child's lives she had gotten to the point she no longer cared and in desperate hope he would finally end her torture and pain she hissed at him in a last attempt at defiance, "If you are going to do then DO IT AND PUT ME OUT OF MY MISERY!" She closed her eyes expecting to feel the sharp steel across her neck.

Shocked at her boldness or perhaps he came to his senses for a second but he unexpectedly released his grip and slumped away into the living room muttering to himself. Sensing the weight lifting from her chest and that something had changed Pippa opened her eyes, and realising she was alone in the hallway she seized the opportunity to open the door and dart through it thinking to escape to a house across the road where she had secretly made a friend of the family there. She felt the cold damp concrete on her bare feet and it seemed to burn her soles with every step, and it seared up her legs. She half ran half waddled across to the terraced red brick house opposite feeling the strain and weight in her abdomen but by the time she reached the tiny porch outside the front door, she barely had time to knock before he caught up with her and again, pinned her again with her back to one wall, the shed door was on her right and the front door of the house was on her left, but this time he did not have a knife in his right hand but the fist was clenched in his anger as he swung with great force aiming for her stomach, he was still threatening her the whole time but she had mentally blocked out his voice, Pippa drew her breath in anticipation and as she did, in that split second time seemed to stand still and she seemed to step back to view the whole scene, yet her body had not moved, she saw the clenched fist coming towards her, she saw it fly through the space where her body occupied yet not make contact with her swollen belly, it was as though her body was no longer a solid mass but some kind of hologram (which is the only thing that could describe the phenomena), yet his fist did make contact with the solid shed door. This made her attacker recoil in pain and step back, it was as though time returned to real time again at that point and the front door had been answered and Pippa looked at her friend who instantly assessed the situation and allowed Pippa in the door. Her friend tried to close the door on Dan but he was too quick and he caught Pippa by her long pony tail and tried to drag her back out the door but Rhoda intervened and in the struggle that ensued managed to get him to release his grip and she slammed the door on him. Rhoda's husband had already dialled 999 and was summoning the police, who could hear Dan's banging on the door and the threats he was spouting and dispatched a car right there and then as details were exchanged.

The two older children were still in the house with her drunken husband so the next thing she had to consider was how she could get them away from him because this time she was determined she was never going back. She could not leave her children with this monster either, she may not be much of a mum but they were better off with her than him! The police arrived shortly after and it turned into a hostage situation and it took hours of negotiation to persuade Dan to let them in to take the children. She and the children were bundled off to a women's refuge in a different town altogether.

That was not the end of that particular trauma but when she was able to recount the event later and thought about it she could come to no other conclusion that a miracle had occurred and from that point on she aware God existed and had preserved her and her child. That was the first time in years she had felt of any worth even if it was only because she might be carrying a child that might be special in some way, and it was what supported her decision and help her determination to get away from this monster once and for all come what may there was no going back. Not least she now knew it was not just her he was prepared to hurt but he was prepared to risk the life of an innocent unborn child.

CHAPTER 19

By the time Pippa and her children had managed to stick it out at the refuge and finally were offered a house of their own, she had thought about that incident and wondered what she should be doing about finding God in her life, as she had been brought up as a Catholic she had little or no understanding of God, who he was or what he was to her, he had always been portrayed as a mystery that us mere mortals would never understand. Nevertheless she tried to connect with the local Catholic Church and even had the children baptised. However the services were repetitive, austere and lacked any kind of connection to her, and taught her nothing about anything other than the dos and don'ts of the Ten Commandments, and how to repeat meaningless phrases when prompted. She found it hard to connect with the people there too as she seemed to have nothing in common with any of them and she felt just as much of a stranger there as anywhere else.

She had been following that routine for about a year when the missionaries from The Church of Jesus Christ of Latter-day Saints knocked on her door. Curious she allowed them in, she had loved the Osmond's and knew they belonged to this church which also added to her curiosity. As the weeks went by and the missionaries explained their doctrine on their weekly visits she felt like all the pieces of the jigsaw that was her life began to fall into place. Finally she had found people who could answer her burning questions about the purpose of life, and she finally understood that she had never been alone in the world as she had thought and that all the bad things that had happened to her had led her to this point where she could finally find and understand her role as a daughter of God. She found a purpose, a hope a future to look forward to which was something she had never felt before and in

1996 she was baptised a member of The Church of Jesus Christ of Latter-day Saints.

Again the Carol came to mind and the hope it inspired, and the bells did indeed peel loud and sweet as she began to be enlightened, and grow in hope and faith.

CHAPTER 20

However many changes took place in the years leading up to her fortieth birthday which was about the same time the kids left home and for the first time in her life she was free to pursue her own interests and full time work was now financially viable.

It took many years of loving care and support by church members, her mum and sister, and much therapy and prayers to get Pippa to come out of her shell once she had escaped the traumas she had been through. She was twenty-six before she was able to feel safe and the nightmares finally subsided. She surrounded herself with friends after attending self -assertive lessons along with the psychotherapy.

She had very little in the way of belongings as she took nothing from the marital home (not that there was anything to take as all Dan's money went on drink and he left her barely able to feed and clothe the children.) She soon learned to be frugal and save to get the things she needed including a washing machine for the very first time in her life, although to be fair the machine was in fact second hand and a payment for some artwork she had done for a company belonging to one of those new friends. Rather than accepting money she settled for some kitchen appliances and other items that the firm were disposing of when they were getting refurbished.

It was then that she realised that in spite of her lack of education she had skills that helped her barter to get the things she needed. She taught herself DIY from library books along with other skills she found she needed in order to get by.

She wanted to go to work but after spending long hours working out as many calculations and wages she could expect given her lack of education and jobs available etc. she came to the conclusion the best she could do at the time was work part time during the day whilst the kids were at school, everything that she earnt over £20 a week was taken off her by benefits but it was surprising how that £20 extra a week helped. She also looked for jobs that paid little more than her £20 allowance, so that her time was spent at home with the children or doing her own DIY and making clothes. Every now and again she was able to sell a painting which helped. In Pippa's mind it was extra and she would try and save half.

As she grew in confidence which was a long process she also realised that she could educate herself by taking advantage of free courses for women which in the 80's there was a big drive towards in Yorkshire. Not all of them turned out to be very useful but she did manage English and word processing which became very helpful. It meant being amongst 16 year olds in the classroom but Pippa was determined to ride it out. For every step forward there seemed to be two steps back and she often got behind or had to give up on a course due to her commitments at home, when she or the children were ill as there was no-one to babysit as most of her friends worked, and felt her place was with the children at those times, so it was tough and things did not run smoothly but she could cope with anything now and she just kept going. They even had the odd trip out together. She prayed constantly for help and although her circumstances did not change dramatically she felt she was being supported by the hand of the Lord she was always able to pay her bills on time and keep the roof over her head. She was thankful and she was free of any threat of violence and as far as she was concerned nothing could ever be that bad again. Her little home was her sanctuary, her safe place. A place where she could grow alongside her children who also showed signs that they had not escaped some psychological trauma from those dark days. Healing was a long process and it helped that being in the church of Jesus Christ of Latter-day Saints meant they were automatically part of a worldwide family full of kind people and she was proud to be one of them. They helped her overcome bitterness, and low self- esteem amongst other things. They showed her how to become a woman with integrity. She learned to forgive, let go and move on. She had the security of knowing there was always someone to help her in a crisis. So to that degree life was good or as good as she felt it could be given her circumstances. She would have been content to continue just getting by and working 9 'til 5 until at a church social she met Lissy…………

CHAPTER 21

Pippa quietly dug in her heals and allowed Lady Bee to throw her weight about like a spoiled child demanding Pippa do as she was told, then, swallowing her feelings of humiliation, and embarrassment and with tears in her eyes she realised she had no choice but to do what Lady Bee was demanding and acknowledged it to her. So when Lady Bee left the room after asserting Pippa would indeed do the washing, Pippa gathered up the wet shirts and threw them defiantly into the washing machine without filling it any further with more items or laundry detergent, she set the dial to wash. "She may have made me do it but it's the last thing I will ever do for her." she thought resolutely to herself, as shaking and frightened she left the room, navigated the stone stairs to her apartment and let herself in, grabbed her coat, mobile phone, and handbag, she took the company car keys out of her bag and left them along with the flat key on her hall table, she was out of there, she needed to think away from the house, she sneaked out her outer door and stairs leading to the side of the manor and to the main driveway, her feet crunching on the pebbles as she walked quickly through the overhanging bushes. It may be a mile or so to walk but she would be at the end of it in no time, before anyone would miss her she would be on the next bus to anywhere it went!

Before she knew it she was on her way home on the train, she had decided she could not go back even to arrange for her stuff to be moved after a couple of hours of deliberating and letting out her tears of frustration and fear. She had spoken to Lissy and told her what had happened. "Well you only had two weeks to go anyway. Sorry it has come to this but it just means you can prepare for a bit longer to come to France. We can sort out a van and go pick up your things at the weekend. Don't worry it will get sorted, even if you were in the wrong she had no right to shout at you or humiliate you in that way it is very unprofessional of her."

"Lord Bee rang me and told me to come back and they would work things out but to be honest, I could not set foot in that place again under the circumstances."

"I can't say I blame you, just get yourself home and I will talk to you later as I have to go now and make the kids lunches, chin up."

"Ok chat later."

Pippa sunk back into the train chair, her mind still whirling with that mornings events. Had she done the right thing? "Well it's done now." She concluded and looked out of the window at the ever changing scenery and tried to think of nicer things and at the same time said a little prayer in her mind and heart. She began to feel at peace once again.

Now all she had to do was think of her new life in France and being her own boss and whatever that might entail it had to be better than being at the mercy of whims of some strange employer!

She drifted into a half sleep with her song of hope playing in her mind.

On her way to her greatest adventure.

SONG OF HOPE Part 2

As I struggled

To find the light

It began to pierce

That blackest night

It grew bigger

And brought to view

Many colours

I thought I knew

I began to hear

The Masters voice

My senses now

No longer void

My grateful heart

Could but praise

Him for these

Glorious rays

To guide my steps

Now quick and sure

To family and

Lonesome pains to cure.

Pressing forward now to better
things.

Karen Leroy has a wealth of unusual life experiences she feels she has to share with others. In non-fictional and fictional format she hopes her experiences can help others in practical and emotional ways. She has already had some success with her first non-fiction 'From Green Fingers to Red Mites 'which encourages people to dive in to the world of growing food, and keeping chickens, and was launched in October 2019.

This is her first venture into fiction which she hopes will be an even bigger success and reach more people that can be helped by this story of endurance and hope. Her message to readers is to keep going no matter how dim the future looks. **It can get better** and everyone's life is precious and purposeful and they are never alone.

Karen's other hobbies include watercolour painting, crafts and fabric design. She has an HNC in art and design.